SBMI

SUBMERSI

Publisher: BoD – Books on Demand, Hellerup, Denmark

Printing: BoD – Books on Damand, Norderstedt, Germany

ISBN: 978-87-4304-720-9

The matted-silver armored caterpillar, designed by the hearts and minds at Aqua Discovery International, prepares its motors and set sails to the crux of the Pacific Ocean. We sail the waveless surface and enjoy for the last time the cloudless heaven, dearly missed during the year-long indoor training sessions. Eventually, we dive down, entering the beautiful liquid world of blue.

Small fishes, their colors lit by the sun's shine in sparkling glow, flow in cooperation with the freshly clean water, making the attention completely unbreakable as we lay eyes onto the glass, viewing the spectacular sights. At least I Martin, did, glancing at my "productive" team from time to time; focusing on the speedy motors rather than equalizing the paperwork with the technical work.

Magical, shining rays slashing down on the water with small fishes going through them, disappearing into their own directions. No aqua talent show can pull off something as glowingly beautiful as that.

Flashes and beeping from all the buttons on the generators are at times like beautiful instruments, but at the same time, screeching cries of chalk on school boards.

The sun's rays slowly vanish from the top, and the small fishes become fewer at the same degree, the deeper we get to the bottom. Rumbling and shakiness falter the iron walls and floor. Thinking not much of it, my yell doesn't penetrate my team's skulls, as every one of them still carries on with their tasks.

> My button-pressing job, as well as holding on to three control levers have both turned obsolete for me. The real job calls from the main dock.

Sprinting towards it, faster than an athlete, I pull the power-lever with hammering force. The rumbling and shaking stop, the speed downwards become spotless.

> Everything erupts into silence. I take a few steps away from the main dock and help my ears and mind to clear every possible thing that could have happened if the lever wasn't pulled in time.

I tell one of my teammates, sitting at the main dock, to adjust the ship's tilt. We sigh in disbelief over our luck, but my teams' frozen glares make me want to vomit, thereafter take a stress pill, and lay down for a very long nap.

About to turn on the engine, a quiet moan near the submarine stops me from pulling the lever. The team have practically turned into ice statues at this point. I ask for a few of them to check all the windows around the ship for any kind of strange activity done outside.

> Fixated to the ocean, I process the moan for what it could be. No ordinary fish moans like that. The lever breathes again as I loosen my sweaty grip.

The team returns with nerve racking results. Nothing unordinary caught their attention as they searched every window. I can't really blame them; the windows are pitch black due to the down warding pace to the bottom. I assure them things will be alright, and the moan was likely some giant, harmless whale scaring us into submersion. They hesitantly continue their work, still glaring at me like frozen statues.

Placing my hand onto the lever to push it, yellowy ovals on the main dock windows swim in sight. Looks to be two gold fishes swimming specific distances from each other.

> Blistering black circles on their stomachs catch me as I get closer. Hard to make out any fins on them. It seems they're not swimming at all. Still.

Frozenly still. I must have blinked six or seven times, since I'm still having difficulties adjusting their bodies, anxiously scanning them with the help of the small lightbulbs we have, in case they aren't normal fishes.

Giant seaweed at the fish's side glide through the dark abyss, floating behind the ovals. There are four of them, at least; thick, long and moving like snakes. Seeing better in the dark, prickly-like cups on them enhances my catching.

They look to be moving mouths; breathing, like jellyfish stuck on the seaweed. It doesn't even seem like their legs are transparent. In fact, there are no legs, not like ordinary jellyfish.

What I feared the most has come back to haunt my ears as a loud, chilling-cold moan triggers all the iron to lose their crippled grips.

Still as a stone, watching in fear as the seaweed smashes the submarine, activating all alarms in every corridor, the gold fishes lift, revealing a giant hole filled with hundreds of razor-sharp teeth, bowing themselves as if preparing to bite at what it's in sight for them. They charge towards the main dock windows and smashes them to shattering pieces. Streams of water pour in, the team panics and runs away from their spots, I follow along. Another glance back at the razors, while my teammate upfront struggles to open the door, the seaweed that passed through the ovals whip themselves from behind and towards the smashed window and the outskirts of the submarine.

> The hundreds of razor teeth and eight seaweed's impact send us flying to the roof, walls, and floor. Myself clutched to the roof, a final impact hurls me downwards, smashing headfirst to the metal floor, blacking me out.

Creaks of metal faintly screams in my ears while water blocks my nostrils every chance I get to breathe. Hesitant to open my eyes, in fear, if this wasn't a nightmare at all. Those gold fishes with black color on their stomachs; seaweed hitting our ship with such force, sending my team and I flying, crashing onto the hard, metal floor; concussing us. Was it all real?

I open my eyes, only for the water to swallow them, igniting my mind back to reality. My feet wobble as I'm trying to stand up and fall to a rail right under my chin, outside of six destroyed generators; wet and smashed, all-colored wires sticking out, sparking the water around them. As I walk on my legs, there's hardly any life in them, like they've been chopped off piece by piece by a chain-saw.

I call out multiple times for my team through the dark-ened, splashed corridors. Both for their help and where-abouts. Splashing water is the only response I get back.

      Despite the pain in my legs, I carefully pull my-self through the rails, on my way to the corridor.

Unable to reach the next rails, I collapse back on the drowning floor, a sledgehammer-like migraine smacks my head. Trying to stop my migraine's banging, the whippings of the water keep me on edge, tiring my arms to the point of being teared off my body.

Managing to grab the other rails, pushing my arms' energy more to the limit, the corridor once again meets my deteriorating glance. This time, nothing will break my concentration. I must get through, to my team, to the main dock. I pull myself more and more upwards, as the submarine keeps tilting for whatever reason.

I manage to take the last rail, holding it for dear life. The ship's up-warding tilt stops, vertically dooming my arms. For every second I hold these rails, the more skin of my arms rips apart on the inside, the outer skin wearing in as the last stronghold. Before my arms truly turn into shredded flesh, the submarine tilts down again, reconnecting every piece of inner flesh in my poor arms.

I let go of the rail, holding my arm shrouded in pain. Even if it was close to be cut by an axe or ripped apart by the heavy gravity make no difference, as I imagine the feeling to be the same.

Splashing through the cold water, with little to no electricity left, I enter the cave-like corridor.

I must be turning blind, the light in the corridor is next to none. In comparison to the room where an unnatural death flashed before my eyes, I could at least make out where I always was.

Entering this corridor is like throwing yourself into an old, dusty cellar with no flashlight in hand. Throat-choking atmosphere and possible presence of a stranger down there cannot be compared to the corridor I'm in right now.

Like that of a cheetah, I spot little light in the corridor. No windows above me where the sun can shine through, nor half-broken lightbulbs to light up the corridor. My eyes have turned into their own lightbulbs.

I make out two pathways in the corridor now. A long one, straight forward. And a short one, at my left. Any hesitation skyrockets away, as I take the left turn but quickly stops. Comfortable thoughts of catching a ladder leading up to the main dock, backfires like a boxing glove filled with bricks on my face, as a disturbing tray downwards to the restrooms is what I spot.

Hard to make out anything, other than faint sights of floating pillows, pieces of mattresses, and yellow sponges floating like dying leaves on a park sea.

The edges of the greenish-blue iron walls are covered in triangular watermarks. The closer I get, the more they appear to pop out of the wall. Getting even closer, small tingles of movement startle my eyes. I glance one more time to the yellow sponge.

Nothing seems out of place, until bigger pieces of sponge contrast the smaller bits. They don't seem square at all, more round-like. Thirteen feet away, they still don't seem off, until... black spots underneath them show up.

I scream in terror, scratching my vocal cords, again hearing that god forbidden moan echo in the metal corridors.

The watermarks are anything but watermarks, they are those giant seaweed from before, or more precisely giant arms, moving like breathing mouths.

Its arms leave slimy liquid marks, raddling like snakes towards me. My steps backwards go slower, both of my legs seem stuck to the ground every time I try to lift them. They constantly fall back down like magnets.

The nightmarish eyes get closer, same goes for its arms sliding towards my feet. As I turn around, about to run back to the corridor to the left side, something thick and soft grabs my right foot, causing me to fall facedown.

One of the four to eight arms block the downward trail, as the giant monster merges itself inside, whipping its arms in all directions in the enclosed air.

I kick the tight arm, only for the grip to tighten on my right ankle, feeling the spongy thickness; no body signal indicating looseness.

Squeezing and turning my foot, hoping for the grip to loosen, I reach down to my pocket and feel a handle. Not like a regular handle on a submarine, more on the lines of a pocketknife. I rush the opportunity and pull the blade at lightning speed and hammers it down on the giant arm, still squeezing every ounce of blood in the veins of my right ankle.

A hysterical, wheezing scream blows my eardrums to the point of deafening me as its grip finally loosens. Managing to get on my feet again, I glance in shock back at the icy cold water; only thing catching my gaze are the yellowy eyes of... that. With a thousand-yard stare, swimming back to the abyss, the darkness masks its eyes of terror and disappears.

The unnatural waves from the water are gone. Praying for it to last forever but fearing it will only last for now, I turn left, still seeing those yellowy eyes before me. They've ruined my night vision and made it impossible for my right ankle to make any shift turns now. The grab from before still feels stuck and trapped, like drowned in acid.

Horrible visions from before halt my pace, making me lean on the cold, iron wall I'm all too familiar with. The snow-like smell freezes all the snot in my nose. I'm picturing two walls at the same side now. They're going in and out of each other like a sniper scope matching its target. The pain in my right ankle increases again, rendering its ability to sprint the same pace as my left ankle impossible. Last bits of progress towards escape's way more difficult than before.

Liquid blows in my nostrils, making me sneeze. Half of the corridor I passed at the beginning is now covered by liquid. I detect the contents of the liquid, strong tastes of salt and old Belgian beer.
The water's closing in. I hammer my right foot again and again. The acid slowly washes away, giving back my foot its natural abilities.

Adjusting to the darkness, loads of bars, like the ones you see in prison cells come into view. Picking up the footing, wobbling towards the bars, I take a hold on the bar at nose height.
Light glimmers my eyes from the top. Resting my cold, dead hand on the bars, I pull myself up, holding onto each bar a chin-bit higher than me. At arms-reach, my

hand touches a cleanly-scraped stone-like floor as I slowly and carefully reach the top.

Huffing and puffing, I pull myself over the last line of bars and rests on the cold stone-like floor.

Liquid drops on my face. This time, thicker and more metallic in a sense.

A scratchy sound turns my attention up to the ceiling; a light bulb with loose wires dangles like a pendulum, barely functioning.

> Despite its lacking functionality, I, clear as day, can make out the scene I have just thrown myself into.

The thick, metallic liquid, red as wine, but tastes nothing like it when blown in my mouth, contrasting the salty taste of the water from downstairs. If the disgusting taste isn't enough, an odor, like one in a shit-covered public toilet but 10 times worse, kills my smelling sense.

> Buzzing flies and worm-like creatures all take their pieces from someone I never knew I would see again, and to my horrifying regret, pricked from head, throat, stomach and legs with holes and scratch wounds, large enough to see intestines, filled with maggots to eat.

My teammate... the one I thought would be the least to end up as food for the ocean's deadly inhabitants lie there. His left eye dangles like the light bulb, blood welling down from his eye socket.

Every ounce of food and beverage hurl up from my stomach, stuck in my throat. Eventually I throw up on the floor, covering my eyes, away from my dead teammate. My heart and mind compete in logical deductions over what's happening and has happened. I want so badly to shake my teammate back to life, but the flies and worm-like creatures will just go after me. I'm going to get out of here and find help for him. No use laying here in this bone-chilling, reddish massacre of a pool and do nothing.
Being in the shoes of a soldier rescuing a dying comrade on the battlefield outside of the trenches at the line of storming fire from the enemy, exactly my position.

Suspecting a new source of beverage and food, the maggots crawl at me; sixty to eighty of them. Like a rabbit jumping from danger, I leap up to a working table, checking my hands for any maggots in the process.

My teammate opens his mouth, and steadily gliding out of the body's mouth is a snake-like tail. No face, nose or even tongue. Crawling more to the side, holding the wall, not losing my glance, the tail rises itself from the corpse and ground.

When reached the ceiling, the tail shows its other side, freezing my body in motionless fear. Prickly cups, moving like breathing mouths.

My wobbly attempt of getting further away ends in semi-success, as my hand touches the air mid-down, my back glides away from the wall and down to the metallic liquid. The haunting tail, skipping through the maggots and table legs, reacts to the splash. It reaches down like a charging eagle about to grab its prey and touches my shoe's tip.

Pushing away, my back becoming one with the door, the tail luckily reaches its limit, still on the tip.

Without much thought, in my desperate intuition, my hand lifts in the air for something to grab as a weapon. Flying in air, it lands on metal, not thick liquid this time, more on the lines of a hard and dry doorknob.

Like capturing an opponent's queen in a game of chess, my hand clings the doorknob and swings it open.

Thrown into another pathway, dark and gritty like the corridor from downstairs, only difference being is a functional lightbulb at the middle. The pathway clouds my eyes from any visibilities like thick fog.

My metallic-liquid hand slides through iron walls, pressing against a holey area of the right side of the wall. Another hard and dry doorknob. When reached, pushing with maximum strength, I throw myself inside.

The safe sights of the lightbulb's rays fade away as the door closes behind me. Claustrophobic darkness strangles my neck, and after loosening my uniform a bit, the stranglehold remains tight. Sounds of thawed meat chewed on at my right.

> Tickling provokes me to scratch my right arm. As I did, it felt like I crushed a bug. Following natural instincts, I pull my fingers slowly away. Strong, sticky creme is the only logical theory I can think of.

A light would be a god's gift to me right now. The tickle from before has worsened, and once again following instincts, I scratch my right arm, but to no end for the tickling.

Better at sensing myself, the tickling is not on my right arm anymore.

It's on my neck.

Blood swirls in my legs, stops at my heart, races in my mind; attempting to lean back on the cold, iron wall to release the tickling, but as I do, squishy, gummy-like pillows, oblong and round have climbed to my back. Barely sliding through the wall, the tickling is back again, though this time I detect movements. I no longer want to know what causes my tickling, as the answer crawls and slides around like jam in the process of being stirred. Only now do I realize what's beside me.

Steadily on my feet, trying not to alert the man-eating colonies, I take off my shirt and start brushing my backside.
Small, squeaky screams die down by every brush, falling to the watered floor and drowns in their sticky blood.

The shirt back in my hand, a sudden flinch makes me drop it. Frantically scratching and hitting my back, something hard and dynamically moving has sunk its teeth in my back; shaking and dangling.

No light needs to shine on the filthy creature that has sticked its teeth into me.

Panicked, able to feel ten meters or more of it, I pull the doorknob faster than running from a school bully threatening you with a knife.

I jump out of the room, landing back first with a miraculous clash, ending with a soft crunch and a terrible rattling noise as I land.

> Squashed hissings roar underneath me as the creature loses its control and after enough hissing, it finally releases its bite. Up on my feet, seeing the snake's teeth gouged in my blood dozes me, having to lean on the wall for support. My head spins like hangovers, every solution in my mind drowns in complicated doubt.
>
> Wobbly gazing at my right, remembering the existence of a left-sided door, I turn the knob and walk inside.

The deadly snake-doze burns in my brain, everything around multiplies in blurring repetitions. Falling on my knees, ready to puke and lie in the vomit and wishing for death, all activity in me shuts off.

I wake up for the second time. Floating around in my blood, the jittering poison from the snake worsens my troubled vision. The lack of light, even in this tiny room, I must get out of here, regardless. If the abyss' task succeeds, I'm well on my way to become a flesh-shredded disciple to the monster.

Amidst the cloudy abyss, an electronic table strikes me. Three thick-squared monitors; black screens with green text in depressing fonts.

> Opened cupboard doors hanging on rusty gold hinges, sleeved and colorful cable wires on the floor. All end-lines pointing to a hole in the wall behind the cabinets.

A shocking revelation lights me up, readying my mind for all exams in the world and vision for obscene scenery. This is the core of the entire submarine.

The main dock was the core of all tilting and power-switching, but this is where the true magic happens.

> A rustling, electrical spark pops inside a bulky computer from IBM; taller and thicker than the rest of the small, dusty office computers from Lenovo, lying all cramped up at the sides and corners of the bulked beast.

The revelation in all its glory hits me with another idea: Communication with Aqua Discovery International.

Aware beforehand of its reverse features during black-outs, always able to send out signals for help if things were to go wrong. Perfect, just what I need. Normally, this should be done by a passenger specifically qualified for code-stuff on the submarine.

A chance to get out of this aqua hell, a burial for my lost teammate, and a stop to this thing taunting me, on the way. Rising from the wet floor, like getting up early in the morning, fresh as the spring breeze which you're normally not, both my hands, locked on the keys, ferociously write down all the possible codes that should work to unlock the computer's reverse-logon.

No response. Only thing spelled out is *error – no connection.*

Up to this point, nothing has worked.

> The lightbulbs, while far from perfect, are the only ones that have worked; paving the way for me to go into this room with all its guidance, despite all the darkness, traumatic sights, and near-death experiences with that hellish creature. All this when I've established contact with the company will be worth it.

Anxiously writing the necessary codes for the reserves is all there is to it now. They just need to send down a help-division, pack my late teammates into body bags, and get me out of here.

A shock from soaked wires beneath while maggots stick their teeth in the millions on me don't matter.

Error again, the reverse code is right on my fingertips.

My fingernails, on the brink of clenching themselves inside my fingers, give away one last performance, producing a code that makes the IBM-computer think for once.

> I put my fingertips to rest, waiting for the computer to process and accept the nail-clenching code.

Reserve Power Granted

Is a message I hope will appear, exactly as I heard it from the directors back at ADI.

Staring at the monitor with those depressive fonts is like a duel in the Old West, the electrical sparks from the computer below the monitor play like music as the stare-down stands.

A new source of music plays outside of the submarine. The moan. After a half-strangled foot, a chokehold in the control room, and now an upcoming stare-down with the familiar terror I've dealt with for a long time now, the next step must be my death.

> Slowly glancing up the window like a student getting verbally bashed by a teacher asking for you to look up, the water, darker than ever; blackness swallowed by pure nothingness.

A startling gliding sound occupies the attention away from the computer's sparking. Figuring out the gliding, while frantically scanning through the right side of the wall-like window, slurpy noises like a plunger being pulled out of a toilet, but on glass with over-the-top force, emanating a startling thud, forcing me to pull back, far away from the windows as possible.
The moan is back but lower this time, stunning every part of me.

Small cyan lamps, hanging on thin threads, dingle side-to-side with sparkling colors like the ones from the surface. Two on the very top. Five to six slightly in the middle, close to the window. And finally, smoothly swimming around at the bottom, remain three last lamps.

> The cyan lamps are surprisingly weak in dissolving the darkness, despite their glimmering

blurred lights. What if they're not actual lamps at all?

Still processing the code, the computer boosts an enormous lust for me to smack the monitor and keyboard, even the computer itself into little pieces with my bare hands, therapeutically relieving all my anxious nerves. What of that moan? Was it coming from the lamps?

Another color, blending with the thin-stringed cyan lamps towers over them. Two reddish circles with an orange-tinted contrast, bigger than any other lamps I've seen move too fast to the window's direction! I duck down and cover my head in a hurry!

> Glass scatters all over the floor, water spurts into the room and hits the computer, breaking it. Two large teeth, shaped like sabers, cut through the thick window, paving ways for huge pools of water to blast into the room. I must be deceiving myself. This creature isn't real... it can't be?!

A giant snake, glancing with fiery red eyes, and a dark moss-green head sliced through the window. Tiny squeaks are the only verbal protests my mouth utters, ability to scream halted.

The snake's sabering teeth penetrates the monitor with the processing code, flickering the display in blizzarding glitches.

Feeling weak but hopeful about a possible defense tool... the colored wires on the water floor!
The massive spits from the window spark the wires back to life, much to my displeasure.

As I run my fingers through the bundle, a spark stings my hand, making me throw it away, not knowing where I threw them exactly.
I rest my electrified hand on my nonelectrified one, clinching the sparks out of my blood vessels.
My grip doesn't hold for very long, as a flashy lightning slash my eyes.
The environment must have left my mind as I threw the bundle away, since something fries.

Hysterical hissings break the windows and crack the monitor's screen even more. The snake pulls its sabers out from the monitor, its teeth and mouth frying due to the ignited insides of the display.

It aggressively swings away from the window and smashes the rest of it with its tail. Nothing more keeping me in here, I storm out.

Slamming the door shut with the water invading the room makes me wish for a burning hot desert to dry out this H2O!

> The right side has proven to be hopeless; the left side is still a semi-mystery. No matter, I'll let my legs do the rest of the talking. Another door, hidden from view until now, appears before me. Ambitions for crushing my eyes can wait, safe checking is the current priority.

Stunned, the five or six of the steps I've taken feel dry. Is this a place the ocean hasn't swallowed already? Another step, still dry.

I stride on the sacred dry floor, sighing deep down in relief; a sigh I never thought I would utter again.

> The blood in my heart flows normally again. Still recovering from mind-boggling anxiety; a tumor of-some-sorts clamming hard onto my brain, crushing every functional channel to a stroke. Being me has never felt greater, but a

metallic rail, eyes not warning me beforehand, smacks my kneecaps as I step right into them.

Falling to the dry floor, agonizing over my aches, I grab the rails and lean over a few meters. The aches go up and down, dreadful in one moment, fine in the next. Another thing my superiors didn't warn me about.

"In case of a near-blackout, watch your every step, or you'll wish you weren't born with knee-caps."

That's what they should have focused much more on. Yeah, the technical aspects are important, but for god's sake, what about the people operating these machines, trapped inside of a matted-silver armored caterpillar? Well, screw them, it's the end-product that truly counts, right? Whatever that "product" may or may not be.

I slide over to the right side of the rails; a secondary dock stare back at me. Nearly all hope has been flushed away, so might as well investigate this dock for any kind of value, not that it really matters anymore.

A buzzling whistle beams in my ears the closer I get to the dock. A radio with a phone hanging by the dock table. On even closer examination, a fluent noise blesses my ears,

"Call Caterpillar 03, this is Aqua Discovery International speaking, what is your status?"

> I can't believe it… an actual voice from someone outside. And as I thought my escape was doomed as soon as that water-basilisk sunk its teeth down to the IBM-computer, there is a little more hope left, thanks to this miracle alone. I snatch the phone.

"This is Martin Davis, attendant and member of Caterpillar 03," I hush out, mind roaring on all things I've witnessed and experienced, "we were attacked by some… sea creature, the entire main dock cracked before my eyes my team died maggots every and another creatur-"

"Wait, wait, hold on a minute, sir. Are you saying you're a member of Caterpillar 03?"

I don't remember anyone outside of our team listed as a member.

"Y-yes, yes, I am. We had just dived and then everything fell apart. There were these yellow eyes and then some giant arms smashed onto our ship."

I fear he may not be able to grasp my situation due to my stammering outbursts, but to my luck,

> "Sir, did you say yellow eyes? What else did you see?" Okay, he's engaged; the least thing I expected.

"Okay, okay... uhm...?" Come on! Think back! Back to where I started! When the entire mission was blown to smithereens.

"I woke up in a generator-like room,"

"Yeah?"

"the ship, while I was trying to inch my way over to, or up to the corridor, tilted upwards! I don't know why? Is that something it does when turned off underwater?"

"I don't think it's supposed to do that, sir. If I'm not mistaken, something enormous outside would be able to do that trick."

Something enormous outside? Now is the perfect time to get to the crux of my story.

"When I got over to the corridor, which was pitch-black by the way, I couldn't see anything. Even the darkest of cellars aren't that dark- "

"I get you, sir, continue!"

"I–I reached two pathways of the corridor and entered left. At first, I only saw sponges from mattrasses and pillows everywhere. That was until I saw yellowy ovals contrasting the sponges, and I realized what it was."

"Yellowy ovals...?"

He quieted down, like he was about to hang up or something. No! I must,

"Eh, hello!? You still there?!"

Back at the other end, he returns, but his voice is abnormally quiet. To a certain degree... lifeless.

"...sir... I–I think what you're up against is exactly what the board of directors were hesitant to tell you and your group. They didn't think it really was– "

  Screeching buzzes blast my ears. No, no, wait! Don't tell me he cut off!?

"Hello! Hello! You there?!" I scream, hands clutched onto the phone, to the point of breaking it a bit.

Can the buzzes just shut up already?! By the time contact has reconnected, I can't hear anything from the other end! The guy would suggest God-given help to me, and I would just stand there, sounding like an idiot and constantly yell "Hello!" every time a suggestion for help is mentioned.

Terrorizing screams overtake every thought of mine, same goes for every desolating hallway in the submarine. I take the phone by its head and smashes it onto the wall where the connector hangs. I strike again and again, emanating and relieving my frustrating anger for every hit. The phone has been turned into ripped, broken pieces of plastic, might as well give it the finishing blow. Just as I do, preparing to give it the final blow, something miraculously calls from it,

"Sir! I've been trying to tell that you that unidentified dots are closing - "
THUD! Lying there on the floor, broken in two pieces, the phone sparks two or three times before shutting off.

I come back to my senses. Staring in shock and utter disappointment at the broken phone. All when everything had lined up perfectly, ready to go, I threw it all away.

My entire upper body catapults on the dock, I scratch and knock my head so many times. Everything's against me... that monster with yellowy ovals could be here any second. The very thing I've been trying to dodge for so long has been rearranged into a linear fashion, thanks to my stupid recklessness.

The remaining rays of hope, vanished. Like a beautiful painting you've spend such a long time to finish and perfect, only for some stupid bastard to spill water over it, ruining its magical aura. And the bastard, out of everyone, is, embarrassingly... yourself.

Clutched on the window like stickers... the same yellowy ovals stare me down. Scared and anxious as I am, I'm not utilizing anymore resistance.
My heart beats left-and-right, urging for the other organs to alarm my brain into action, but drowns and gets abandoned by the blood of my stubborn subconscious.

Here I am, standing in the middle, arms raised; allowing those devilish ovals to take me over. The ovals fade away, only to go back again. It's like they're covered by a giant tail.

It's not seaweed, but a thick-skinned tail. The yellowy ovals emancipate themselves from the long tail, tricking a window-splitting slither from it. Both ovals pull away, as if something has wrapped it from behind. Closer, two reddish lamps with orange-tinted contrasts appear at the sight of the yellowy ovals and push the body of the ovals towards the window.

Cracks and shards of glass strike at my direction. I throw myself at the side of a metallic wall with a small window and shoot my glance to the giants, where an arm of the ovals whips the entire room, smashing monitors, the floor and, to my greatest dismay, the rails keeping the generators safe that recently smacked my kneecaps.

The giant arm's prickly cups suck themselves to the generators, and with such barraging force, explode the generators into intimidating sparks, way more intimidating than the shock against the snake.

> Lightning bolts spurt out and hit my already-sparked right hand, causing me to lay sideways. My hand's blood boils and streams from wrist to fingers.

In swooshing speed, the ovals hurl their giant arm out, removing the blockade I took too much for granted. Devouring waterfalls spurt into the secondary dock room, drowning half-side of my body, still holding onto my sparked hand.

I get on my knees, forcing them to comply with my on-the-spot escape plan. Suffer now, relax later, I keep repeating. The ovals and lamps are next-to-none, as the darkness of the ocean swallows them whole. Claustrophobia is wearing off, they're not in sight of my hearing now, time for the hallway-door to be teared to shreds.

> My fried rosin-hands rips the doorknob and out comes the waterfall from the other side, one blinding my body whole; eyes, ears, nostrils, and mouth choked away into the abyss.

I can't breathe. Water has annexed my nose, the pole opposite of the enclosed air I had otherwise come to terms with; suppressing my eyeballs like thick fingers penetrating my skull, the only parts I can truly feel. My migraines are gone thanks to the painkilling power of the abyss, but my legs and arms are unbelievably numb.

> Though smearing my face like a massage after a long sun-burned walk through a city the size of an empire, the rumbling water puts my anxiety to levels of utter helplessness.

Swirling glides spin around my leg and upwards to the waist, reminding me I still had legs despite the numbness. The glides stop and clenches my left leg. It feels like ten or fifteen mouths, each sinking hundreds of small, razor-sharp teeth into my thigh and shin. Moving in square inches the best I can do tightens the clench more.

The loud moan of those yellowy ovals fighting the reddish lamps, screams right in my face like blowing storms, escalating the eyeball-penetrating fingers' hold on me. If I scream, the very little air in me will be the least of my worries compared to the crushing strength of the gliding, keeping me stuck.

Like in slow motion, my right foot puffs the surrounding glides and regretfully get stuck the same way as the leg it tried to rescue. Another moan screams at my face, tightening its grip from the right foot to the waist. The spin of mouths swirls around, clenched, and tight like a belt for a small child.

> The source of the belts repeats the formation through my uniform, around my arms, and onto my throat like a necklace of death. All belts tighten, pressing the last bit of air which still blows in my lungs.

Sudden, slow movements by the tight belts pan my legs in opposite sides. Further away, the outskirts of my thighs cramp, clamming the waist-side of my legs like knotted wires. Even further, the inner parts rip like pulling on a bag until it splits open by force.

As the last thing I pledged not to do, my mouth fires open, as both of my legs shred. A warmer sort-of water lays like a flying duvet over my face. I shut my mouth close in an instant, and immediately tastes the thing I never could have said without feeling very sick or fainting. Blood. My own blood.
I squeeze and scratch the giant razor belts, and meet again that warm water, hitting my left side this time. I kick and try to find a loophole to loosen the tight belts. As I kick, one final shred freezes me. The warm water now covers my face like thirty duvets.

The other gives one last boot, another freezing, and another thirty duvets covering my face. Relaxing rumbling's breach fall on my unfortunate deaf ears. Exploded with warm and cold water, my eardrums have heard their last song, the worst song I've ever heard. Blizzarding whistle are somehow the only song playing now... but... how...? My ears are gone... how tragic... tragic... tragic...

I've been sitting here for half an hour, staring at my sound recorder laying before me on the table, collecting every thought, positive and negative. I press on the start button, thinking of starting off with an overview.

"My name is Damon Tristan. The clock is close to 9 pm. Six hours ago, I booked out from my company, and let the fresh, summer air undertake their everyday therapy through my veins, after a good six hours in front of my blocky computer screen. But the air that entered my veins as I stuck my keys into my car were filled with re-gret, despair, disappointment, sorrow, and... foolish-ness."
Swallowing spits of the five mentioned-emotions, I con-tinue.
"I work as a communication supporter at Aqua Discovery International. My job is to take calls and help as many people as possible. From customers, trainees, certain key managers if something on their systems don't work properly, and most importantly, divers; the ones doing the dirty work.

A diver goes through a year-long practice run, studying the technical capacities and capabilities of ships. Mostly submarines. There is a common phrase known too well in the diver-circle, 'We start off big, we finish off small.' Last year, a team consisting of precisely forty people were put into training. On the final day, only seven remained. Before we knew it, the deadline was among the divers. The one that... urgh...what now..."

A phone at my right rings, interrupting the important part of my recording. Hesitant to take it, I pause the recorder and grab the phone. It's from a man, calm as a family therapist, but cold as a John Doe. He refuses to tell me his name, but rather tells me this,

"I know what you're planning to do, Damon, and that's something we simply cannot allow you to do."
I'm close at slamming the phone back to its base. It feels like it's burning my fingers. But I need to know more about him, so I pull it back.
"I w-wasn't going to anything, I promise..."
"You can take that lie and shove it in the bullet resting in my friendly tool as we speak."

I glance at my window, nothing but pitch blackness.

"It's no use, Damon, just like it was no use helping Martin escape that submarine earlier today. I bet it got him."

One more word from him and I swear I will storm out the door and shut him up myself if he mentions him one more time.

"Why this...? Why sent all these people down there?! You, yourselves have no idea what it even is!"

Small pauses must mean I've gotten through his skin now. Yet,

"We do, Damon. We've done so since the company first started sailing the Pacific Ocean."

"But... but why would- "

"You have a duty of confidentiality, Damon, I sincerely hope you haven't forgotten that?"

"No, no I haven't- "

"We've also covered it all up. Said it was a horrible accident. The family of his have already been compensated. The same goes for the others."

I'm ready to end the conversation now, and in my crying heart and angry mind, I say,

"I will tell the truth. And nothing but the truth... sir."

I lower the phone, ready to hang up, ready to tell the truth to everyone.

"I guess my disguise didn't go in vain, after all. Wouldn't you agree?"
"The what?!- "
The pitch blackness outside the window emerges itself, revealing a cold glare of a man dressed in all black except his face. The man pulls out, from at first glance seems like a shiny, silver baseball bat. One last glance, and I see for what it is.

A pistol, pointing at my face.

I'm sorry I failed my task as a communication supporter, and sorry I let all those people down. Sorry, everyone...

sorry, Martin...